Pony Camp
P C
Diaries

Millie and
Magic

D1420129

SEFTON LIBRARY SERVICES

002716494	
Bertrams	21/10/2010
JF	
M	£4.99

0 027 164 94X XB

Other titles in the series:

Megan and Mischief
Poppy and Prince
Chloe and Cracker
Sophie and Shine
Charlie and Charm
Emily and Emerald
Lauren and Lucky
Jessica and Jewel
Hannah and Hope

www.kellymckain.co.uk

THIS DIARY BELONGS TO

☆ Millie ☆

Dear Riders,

A warm welcome to Sunnyside Stables!

Sunnyside is our home and for the next week it will be yours, too! My husband Johnny and I have two children, Millie and James, plus two dogs ... and all the ponies, of course!

We have friendly yard staff and a very talented instructor, Sally, to help you get the most out of your week. If you have any worries or questions about anything at all, just ask. We're here to help, and we want your holiday to be as enjoyable as possible – so don't be shy!

As you know, you will have a pony to look after as your own for the week. Your pony can't wait to meet you and start having fun! During your stay, you'll be caring for your pony, improving your riding, learning new skills and making new friends. Add hacks in the countryside and a gymkhana at the end of the week, and you're in for a fun-packed holiday to remember!

This special Pony Camp Diary is for you to fill with your holiday memories. We hope you'll write all about your adventures here at Sunnyside Stables – because we know you're going to have lots!

Wishing you a wonderful time with us!

Jody xx

8.30 on Monday morning

Hi, Millie here! It feels strange to be starting a Pony Camp Diary of my own. The reason I'm writing one is that, for this week only, I'm going to be a Pony Camp girl! As well as taking part in the lessons and gymkhana, I'm joining in all the lectures and yard work. It was Mum's idea. She's arranged for me to try out a new pony, and if it works out they'll buy him for me. She thinks if I take part in all the activities, we'll get a chance to really *bond*.

Yeah, right!

As if I could bond with anyone but my lovely Tally! We're a team, him and me.

The problem is, Mum's convinced that my gorgeous cheeky chops is too small for me. I've tried and tried to tell her he isn't, but she won't change her mind. She kept going on about it until she somehow persuaded me to give another pony a try.

The new pony's called Magic and he belonged to the daughter of a friend of hers. He arrived yesterday evening and we turned him out into a field with the others. He fitted in really well, making friends with Charm and Jewel straight away – after five minutes they were all grazing happily together.

But when Tally trotted up to say hello to me as usual I felt SO guilty. I know I agreed to try

Magic

out Magic (in the end!), but that doesn't mean I'm happy about it.

Magic *is* lovely and all that – he's an elegant bay thoroughbred cross. And you can tell he has a good temperament. Mum says his paces are perfect, too.

But no pony could replace Tally. He's not perfect, but he's got, what's the word –

Us two have had some amazing adventures – razzing round the cross-country course, galloping on hacks and doing *loads* of jumping. True, I have been dragged through a hedge or two when he gets a little – ahem – "over-enthusiastic", but I don't mind that.

Anyway, Mum's wrong about Tally. I'm not *that* big for him. I'm sure we could have another year together; well, six months at least – and after that we could get into driving. But Mum doesn't agree, so I'm going to have to put Operation Keep Tally into action. Not that I've got an actual *plan* yet, not really, not a decent one.

This is all I've come up with so far:

OPERATION KEEP TALLY

PLAN A
Make Tally bigger

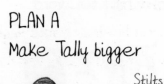

Stilts

Jodh boots
on my knees

PLAN B
Make myself smaller

PLAN C
Run away together
Probably not a good idea 'cos:

1. We'd have to sleep
in hay barns and fields,
and what if a farmer
let out an angry bull?

2. I'd miss out on Mum's roasts
with Dad's Yorkshire puddings
  and
3. I suppose Mum and Dad would
miss me a bit (and my big bro James might
too, even if he is a smelly-pants who gives
me dead arms for no reason).

See, rubbish or what?!
Oh, hang on, I've thought of another one.

PLAN D
Maybe me and Tally could chain ourselves
together as a protest.
   But what if I need the loo, or even
worse, what if Tally does?!

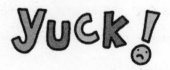

Mum's just walked past and given me a big smile. She thinks I'm getting into the spirit of things, writing in here already (I'm not *into* writing, normally). But she doesn't know what I'm really using this diary for – which is to report on Operation Keep Tally – hee hee!

Oh, gotta go, this week's girls are starting to arrive. They're all loud and lively and chattering away as usual. I SO love living here – it's like being on holiday all the time. And James has gone to an outdoor adventure camp, which makes it even better. I wonder who I'm sharing my room with this week? I hope they don't snore!

Monday after lunch,
outside on the picnic tables

Well, what a shock! You won't believe
what our instructor Sally's done. She's
only gone and given Tally to one of the
Pony Camp girls. Yes, as in to be her own pony
for the week. OK, so I know I'm riding Magic,
but it's only supposed to be a trial. Now it feels
like everything's already been decided. I can't
believe she's done that! I bet *Mum's* behind this!

In cahoots!

Sally   Mum

I suppose I should do the same as my room-
mates, Amy and Zoe, which is write down all
this week's girls and ponies.

Sunnyside Stables

Angelika + Jewel

Zuzanna + Charm

Irenka + Flame

Zoe + Fisher

Amy + Mischief

Evie + Prince

Elizabeth + Amber

Kasia + Tally (?!?)

I was going to draw Kasia looking like a
meanie after stealing MY pony, but I didn't 'cos:

1. She's really nice

and

2. It's not her fault she was given Tally.

Kasia (you say it Ka-sha) is Irenka's little sister,
but she's sharing with Evie and Elizabeth, the
two girls from Devon. That's because Irenka's
two friends Angelika and Zuzanna have come
too, and they're all sharing. (They're all Polish
but they live in London, not Poland itself.)

I'm sharing with Zoe and Amy, who are
sitting here now, writing *their* diaries. They're
both 10, like me. Amy's really chatty and bubbly
and Zoe's quieter and so smiley. They'd already
put their stuff in my room, but we got properly
chatting as we had the tour round Sunnyside.
I found out that Zoe's from one bit of London
(Ealing) and Amy's from another bit (North
Finchley). They both go to different city riding

stables where they have to stay in the manège, so they can't wait to hack out in the open countryside.

But my excitement STOPPED when we went back to the yard and Lydia led the ponies out ready for the assessment lesson. I tried to smile when she handed me Magic's reins, but then *Tally* came out and my stomach lurched. I must have been staring in horror as she gave him to Kasia because Zoe asked me if I was OK. So I had to tell her and Amy he was my pony, but I just whispered it really quietly in case Kasia heard and it upset her. Zoe went,

"Oh, that must feel a bit funny. Are you OK about someone else riding him?"

I shrugged. "I guess it's fine," I replied. Then I got Amy talking about the ponies at her riding school to change the subject.

In the assessment lesson, Sally put me at the front, for some annoying reason. That meant I had to keep twisting around to check on Tally, which made Magic think I wanted him to *turn*, so we kept going off the track. I knew Tally was confused and upset, seeing me riding another pony, and that made me feel even worse. When he kept trying to cut the corners off, I called out, "I think he wants to catch up and see me." I hadn't meant to say that, but it just came out before I could stop myself.

POOR Tally!

"Why?" Kasia asked, so then I had to say he was mine in front of everyone. Kasia looked a bit surprised.

"He's just being lazy, that's all," Sally told me. Then she said to Kasia, "Don't be afraid to kick on and really steer into the corners, so he can't get away with it."

Well, that put me in a grump! I mean, I think I know how my own pony feels! But I didn't say anything – Sally's a fab instructor and we get on brilliantly (usually!) so I didn't want to annoy her.

Magic's a different shape to Tally and I just couldn't seem to find a comfy position for my legs. While I was busy fiddling with my stirrups, Sally called out, "Off you go with Magic!" about five times. It took me ages to realize she meant *me*, so I held everyone up. And even worse, whenever she said "Tally" I kept thinking she *did* mean me and setting off into trot or whatever.

Then as we were changing rein across the school at E I was trying to explain to Kasia that Tally won't turn sharply unless you really get your leg on and push him round from behind. Sally called out, "Millie, I am the instructor round here, thank you very much, and Kasia is doing just fine. All the girls have to learn about their new ponies and perhaps you should do the same with Magic, instead of worrying about other people."

How embarrassing!

And anyway, how *could* I think about Magic when poor Tally had no idea what was going on? And he didn't even get a canter, because when Sally gave us the choice, Kasia decided to stay in trot. I couldn't help blurting out, "But we've been plodding along all lesson. Tally's desperate for a good razz round."

"Even more reason for Kasia to stay in trot!" Sally cried. "And stop interfering, Millie!"

She looked *really* annoyed with me then, so I forced myself to zip my lips.

As Tally trotted round behind Prince and Evie, he looked so miserable, and I wished I could explain to him that none of this was my idea!

stuck in trot!

Zoe decided to stay in trot too, and went round behind Amber and Elizabeth. She's got a really good seat for someone who hasn't ridden much, and I'm sure she'll be whizzing along soon enough.

CHEEKY Boy!

Amy cantered on Mischief and she was really confident, although he did cut the corner and drop into trot a couple of times, then do a big plunge when she asked for canter again. Typical of him! He's so cheeky! I think he was hoping to send her flying, but she held on and kept trying till she got him going nicely. Good for her! Me and Zoe said a big well done to Amy after the lesson, and she was really pleased with herself.

Angelika and Zuzanna are brilliant riders, and Irenka's really good too, considering she's only

been riding two years, the same as Kasia.
Although she's not that experienced, she's really
brave. Like, when Flame decided that canter
wasn't fast enough and absolutely *bolted* down
the long side, Irenka screamed and I thought
she'd refuse to try again. But Sally got her to
ride a couple of circles in trot then asked for
canter, and Flame went calmly that time (well,
as calmly as she ever goes!).

Magic was easy to get into canter and had a
nice even rhythm. And we made such a smooth
downward transition you could hardly see me
do anything. Mum's right, he *would* make
someone a lovely pony – it just won't be me!

When we got back to the barn to untack,
everyone was chattering excitedly about the
lesson, and telling me that I'm SO lucky to live
here – as usual! I managed to smile and say,
"Yes, I am," but it was quite hard to watch Kasia
brushing Tally down.

Lydia

He looked as sad as me, so when Kasia took his water bucket off to the yard to scrub out and fill up, I went over and gave him a big hug.

And guess what?

Lydia saw and told me off!

Huh! I hadn't even noticed she was there! She said, "Tally's fine, Millie, stop fussing. Poor Magic needs a bit of attention, though."

Well, he looked perfectly OK to me, but I went back into his pen and brushed him anyway, just to keep her happy. His coat came up really well, and he was so still and calm, I didn't even have to watch my feet. He's a real sweetie and, like I said, I'm sure he'll make someone a great pony.

Amy was so funny at lunch just now, doing an impression of Mischief trying to plunge her off. Me and Zoe were in stitches watching her canter around the picnic tables.

Then when I was finishing off my fruit salad and ice cream I came up with a new plan for Operation Keep Tally. It's way better than any of the silly ideas I had before, but I'm keeping it to myself, in case my new mates accidentally let something slip (especially loud-girl Amy!). In fact, I'm moving my arm over this page, so they don't read anything!

OPERATION KEEP TALLY
NEW IMPROVED PLAN A
— RIDE BADLY
If Mum and Sally think I can't
ride Magic very well, maybe
they won't let me have him and
I'll get to keep Tally instead.
Ta-daaaaa! Genius or what?!

Oh, Sally just came in and announced the
groups. I'm in Group B with Amy and the
older girls, and Zoe's in Group A with Evie,
Elizabeth and Kasia (on MY pony). It's time to
go down to the yard now. Fingers crossed that
my plan goes well!

Monday after tea

The lecture this afternoon was on tack and tacking up. In the tack room Sally was pointing to all these different things and we had to say what they were. I made sure I was first to put my hand up, and I mentioned Tally every time, so she'd know how much I was missing him. "That's a standing martingale, which could be useful on a lively pony like *Tally*, if he got into the habit of throwing his head up," I called out. And, "That's an eggbutt snaffle bit, which should be fine for most ponies, but you might want to use a drop or flash noseband with it rather than a cavesson if you've got a headstrong one, *like Tally*." I thought Sally would be pleased that I was doing so well, but after a while she just said, "OK, thanks, Millie. Let someone else have a go now."

Double embarrassing! I must have looked like
a right show-off, and I hadn't even realized it.

Once Sally had done a demo on Prince on
the yard, we had to have a go at tacking up for
ourselves. I was first back into the tack room
and without even thinking about it, I lifted
down Tally's saddle and bridle. When I turned
round, I found myself face

to face with Irenka
and Kasia. Whoops!
I honestly took it
by accident, but it
must have looked
strange. "Sorry, erm,
I just got this down out
of habit," I muttered, heaving the saddle into
Kasia's arms and hanging the bridle on her
shoulder. She said thanks, but Irenka gave me
a funny look, like she thought I was trying to
take over.

With Magic tacked up,
I was all set to put my new
plan into action. As we
walked our ponies around
the track to warm up,
I dropped my toes down
and let my arms go floppy.

"Sit up, Millie, you look like a sack of
potatoes!" Sally called.

Good! I thought. I also made sure we kept on
wandering forward when I reached the markers
for halt, I turned our circles into wonky egg
shapes, and I let Magic poke his nose out and
stray off the track. Not surprisingly, we kept
getting corrected and having to try things again.
And I made sure we did an even worse job the
second time round – hee hee!

And when we did some jumping I didn't
even have to *try* to ride badly. It turns out that
Magic gets nervous when the heights go up and

stops dead. He might have got over with some encouragement, but of course I didn't give him any and he kept refusing. Even better, Dad stopped by the fence to watch, so *he* saw me being hopeless with Magic, too!

After about the fifth go, Sally called out, "Millie, you're not even trying! You can't expect every pony to leap over like Tally does! I just don't know what's got into you!"

"Sorry," I mumbled, but really I was thinking, *Great, she's already seen that me and Magic aren't right together, now she just needs to tell me that and job done.* So as we were dismounting in the yard I said to her, "Oh, what a shame that I found everything so much more difficult on Magic than Tally. He's just not—"

Sally looked at me wearily. "Don't blame the pony, Millie," she said. "Look at the rider."

"But I—" I began.

"You need to pay attention to what Magic

needs, rather than just automatically riding the same way you'd ride Tally," she said sternly. "You have to put more effort in, really *try*. You and Tally had obviously got stuck in a rut and you've let your skills slide. I should have noticed that before. Thank goodness you've got a new pony to wake you up a bit!"

"But I…" I said again, then trailed off. I couldn't tell her I'd ridden badly on purpose – she'd be so cross, and she'd definitely tell Mum. I've told them enough times that I want to keep riding Tally, and they've always said no. Somehow I've got to make them think it's *their* idea. But this plan has seriously backfired, and I don't have another one. What on earth am I going to do?

Oh, here come Amy and Zoe, gotta go.

10.27p.m. on Monday

I'm writing this by the light of my torch. We were planning to stay up till midnight whispering, then sneak down to the kitchen and raid the treats tin, but in the end Zoe and Amy were fast asleep by ten fifteen. They were really tired because they're not used to so much riding!

Us three had such a laugh tonight playing on the dance mats, and sitting at the kitchen table chatting and making mini-marshmallow patterns in our hot chocolates.

Then when we were snuggled up in our beds before lights out, I ended up telling them all about Tally, like how we won last year's Crewkerne Show cross-country comp, and how he loves riding into the sea when we go to the beach, and how cute he is when he tries to

stick his head in my pocket
to look for Polos.
"I miss him so much
and I'm desperate to
get him back," I finally
admitted.

Tally

I was hoping they'd be able to help me come
up with another plan to keep him, but they
didn't. Instead, Zoe said, "Mil, you really ought
to talk to your mum about this. Perhaps she
doesn't realize how strongly you feel."

"That won't work because she won't take
any notice, as usual," I grumbled.

"But perhaps she'll listen when she realizes
how serious you are about keeping Tally," said
Amy. "It's got to be worth a try."

So I'm going to do it. After all, I don't have
any better ideas, and if I don't do something
soon I'll lose my gorgeous Tally for ever. Maybe
they're right and Mum *will* understand.

Tuesday — I'm just quickly writing this before lunch

Well, I did try to talk to Mum after breakfast, but she was too busy clearing up and finding lost boots and gloves as usual. I tried again when we had our break for squash and biccies, but she was called to the phone. Then I tried *again* when she was getting Group A mounted up for her lesson, but she kept asking me to give leg-ups and adjust stirrups, and didn't listen properly. So I gave up in the end.

In the barn before the lesson, I was getting the mud off Magic's legs and I went into a daydream thinking of Tally, brushing and brushing away. I only came out of it when Zoe shook my shoulder and said, "I think you've finished." I blinked down at Magic's legs and saw they were gleaming. Tally's always take so long I'd just assumed Magic's would too. So because

I had time I went to help Kasia. I was just
pointing out where she'd missed some bits of
mud when Sally came over and said, "What's
going on here?"

"Millie's helping me do Tally's legs," Kasia
replied.

Sally raised an eyebrow at me. "I bet she
was," she said. I noticed then that Irenka,
Zuzanna and Angelika were looking at me too,
in an annoyed way. Maybe they all thought I
was taking over and not letting Kasia do things
for herself, but really it wasn't like that. I just
wanted Tally to be thoroughly groomed. Little
clods of mud like that can be uncomfortable
when they dry.

"I should really get back to Magic now,"
I mumbled and hurried off, before Sally could
say anything else.

In the lesson this morning Sally wanted to
give the older girls a challenge because they're

picking things up really quickly, so we tried
some lateral work. Magic was really good at leg
yield and soon got the hang of shoulder in, too.
(I didn't bother riding badly today because it
didn't work yesterday.) I kept thinking he was
going to get bored and go bolting off or bucking
about, like Tally would, but he really listened to
me and just kept trying and trying.

I was actually enjoying it, until Sally said,
"Well done, Millie. I bet you never dreamed
you'd get to do this kind of thing. It's not Tally's
cup of tea, but with Magic, you're doing
brilliantly!" I suddenly felt guilty for
having fun with Magic, so I very
loudly said, "I actually *like* being
dragged around the manège by
Tally. At least he's got personality.
Magic's such a Mr Perfect, it's boring."

Mr Perfect!

"Well, I think he's fab," Irenka said, taking me
by surprise.

That's when I realized how spoilt I sounded.
My stomach lurched and I tried to speak, but no
words would come out. I felt terrible. I hadn't
meant to put Magic down, only to defend Tally.
"I know he is," I finally managed to mumble.
"I wasn't saying he's not, but… Oh, it's just…
Never mind."

Afterwards I was in the barn with Zoe and
Amy, and I was just asking Zoe how Kasia and
Tally got on in the lesson, when I realized Irenka
was standing right behind me. "Do you have a
problem with my sister riding Tally?" she asked.

I blushed bright red and gaped at her. I felt
so awkward again. It's like everyone keeps
misunderstanding everything I do.

"It's not Kasia's fault
she got him," she
said. "You
shouldn't take it
out on her."

"But I'm not!" I finally managed to croak.

"Well, stop interfering then," said Irenka crossly, and marched off back to her friends.

"I was only trying to help," I barely-whispered, but she was too far away to hear. My heart was hammering and I felt a bit trembly. Zoe put her arm round me, and Amy said, "You all right?"

I nodded, although I wasn't, not really.

"I can understand why she's got the wrong idea, Mil," said Zoe gently. "Look, have you spoken to your mum about Tally yet?"

"I've tried!" I cried. "Three times! But she's so busy."

"No excuses," Amy said firmly. "Tell her at lunchtime. This is important. You have to MAKE her listen."

So that's what I'm going to do. It's nearly time to go in now, so here goes…

Tuesday afternoon

Well, I'm sitting at the kitchen table with an ice pack on my ankle, and EVERYONE is cross with me.

If Mum hadn't been too busy to listen to me again I wouldn't have got so mad, and if I hadn't got so mad then…

But no, I know this is no one's fault but my own. I don't even want to write down what happened, not really, because I feel so bad about it. But I'm stuck here by myself with nothing to do, so I might as well.

When I went up to Mum again to tell her how I felt, she was stirring a pan of soup while rummaging in the cupboard for the side plates, with her mobile clamped between her ear and shoulder, on hold to someone. As I started speaking she tried to give me the plates, saying, "Put these out, would you, love?" But I wouldn't take them. I just stood there with my arms folded. I wasn't giving up this time.

As Mum hung up the phone, I took a deep breath. "I really miss Tally," I began. "Would it be OK if I had him back next week?"

Mum sighed and clattered the plates down on the side. Then she opened the cutlery drawer and said, "I thought you liked Magic?"

"I do, it's just that—"

"No, Millie," she said, chopping a pile of carrots into sticks now. "We've talked about this. A *lot*. You're just too big for Tally. And besides, it's only Tuesday, you've hardly even given Magic a chance."

"But I have and he's not right for me," I insisted. "I want Tally back. I can't believe you just gave him to one of the Pony Camp girls without even asking me!"

"Millie!" Mum snapped. "Can't you see I'm trying to get lunch on the table? Let's talk about this later when there's time—"

"There's never time!" I shouted, and stormed out.

After that, I was just so angry and upset that I wasn't thinking straight. I thought I'd never get the chance to ride Tally again. That's why I came up with such a completely stupid idea.

As the girls passed me on their way in to lunch, all chatting and laughing, I grabbed Zoe and Amy by the hand and pulled them back outside. I told them what I was planning and begged them to cover for me. "Just tell Mum I've gone to share Dad's sandwiches in the yard office," I said. Amy was fine about it, but Zoe didn't want to at first. "It's no big deal," I insisted. "I'm just going to take Tally up to the cross-country course and pop over a few fences. I'll have him back and untacked before anyone notices. I'll probably even be back in time for pudding. Please, Zo, this is really important to me." She still wasn't sure, but she did promise not to say anything to Mum in the end.

I wish I could go back in time and change things, but it's too late now.

I sneaked off, keeping an eye out for Lydia and Dad, but there was no one around. Tally's saddle and bridle were still hanging on the rail in the barn, along with the others. I tacked him up quickly, ruffling his mane and whispering how much I'd missed him. He nuzzled my shoulder and I knew he'd missed me too. I heaved myself into the saddle and off we went. My heart skipped a beat as I saw Lydia coming out of the feed room, but she didn't look our way, thank goodness.

We trotted up the lane and through the gate into the far field, where the cross-country course is. We warmed up for a bit then did a couple of circuits of the hedge and gate, then over the tyres and ditch. It was great to be riding Tally again, and I could tell how much he was enjoying having a good razz around.

Then we did the log pile, hedge and ditch combo. It was fun but we'd done it so many times before...

We'd never tried the high part of the log jump, though.

I'd always thought me and Tally could manage it, if only we'd been allowed to try. I'd asked Sally a few times, but she'd always said no and made me stick to the low side. But Tally's got such a bold jump I was sure we could clear it. I circled a couple of times and jumped the low half as usual. We sailed over, easy-peasy. The high bit couldn't be *that* different, could it?

"Millie!"

The shout made me glance up. Not Mum –
phew! Zoe and Amy. I must have lost track of
time, because they'd snuck up here at the end
of lunch to tell me it was nearly time to go back
on the yard.

"Hey, watch this!" I shouted.

I kicked Tally on, really letting him go. In
hindsight, I should have kept him more
collected, and thought about *power*, not
speed. Now that we were thundering towards
the jump, the high side looked *very* high.

Tally jumped long and flat. His front legs hit the solid log and he scrabbled over, only just managing to get his feet down at the other side and avoid falling on to his shoulder. I went flying, of course. I landed weirdly on my ankle, then my chest hit the ground and all the breath was knocked out of me.

I heard my friends shouting my name and it seemed to take them for ever to reach me.

"I'm OK," I croaked, but then, "Ow!" I yelped, as I tried to move. My ankle hurt so much I thought it must be broken. Wincing with pain, I pulled myself up to sitting, then scanned the field for Tally.

My stomach lurched when I saw he was limping. I'd been in such a hurry to get out here without being spotted that I hadn't even bandaged his legs. That knock must have hurt so much. I couldn't believe how stupid I'd been. I called to him, but he wouldn't come to me.

Tally!

"Let's get you up," said Amy. She looked really worried. They both did. She slipped her arm under mine on one side, and Zoe did the same on the other. They heaved me to my feet, but my legs were trembling so much that I collapsed back into a heap on the grass.

That's when Zoe got really scared and went running back to get help.

After a while, Zoe came dashing into the field with Mum. Mum fell on to her knees and pulled me into a hug. "Thank goodness you're OK!" she gasped. Then… "How dare you come out here by yourself! What a stupid, stupid thing to do. How could you be so irresponsible?!"

I don't think I've ever seen her so angry.
Amy and Zoe just looked at the grass,
probably hoping she wouldn't turn on *them*.
Then Dad came running up with Sally. He
looked almost as angry as Mum. I tried again
to get up, but my ankle throbbed so much it
made me gasp. "It's OK, I've got you," said
Dad, lifting me into his arms.

"I'll get Tally," said Sally.

"I hope he's OK!" I stuttered.

"So do I," she said grimly, then hurried off.

When we got into the kitchen, all the
other girls were gathered by the
door, waiting to go down to the
yard. They all gasped when Dad
burst in, carrying me, and started
asking what happened and if I was
OK. I winced with pain as Dad put me
down in a chair, but insisted that I was fine.

Then Mum examined my ankle. "You're very

lucky, Millie," she said gravely. "It's just bruised.
I'll get you an ice pack. Now, Lydia, could you
go and help with Tally, please?"

"Tally?!" Kasia cried. She looked at me
in astonishment. "But what were you doing
on Tally?"

"Well, I just thought…" I began.

"You didn't think, that's the point," Mum
snapped, and I decided it was probably better
not to say anything after that. I tried to pretend
I hadn't noticed Irenka and her friends all giving
me angry glares.

Sally came in then.

"How is he?" Dad and I both asked at once.

"I think it's only a strain, but I'll call the vet
out just to be on the safe side," she told us.
Then she turned to Kasia and said, "I'm afraid
you won't be able to ride him this afternoon,
and we'll have to wait and see about the rest
of the week. I'm sorry, love."

Kasia looked so upset. I didn't think she'd be that bothered about Tally, not when she'd only been with him for two days. But she really was, and I felt even worse.

"I'm so sorry, Kasia," I said, but she didn't reply. Irenka put her arm round her sister and suddenly *everyone* was staring angrily at me. Not just Irenka and her friends, but Kasia's room-mates Elizabeth and Evie, and Dad and Sally too.

Lydia smiled at Kasia. "Don't worry, sweetie," she said, "I'll go and get Cracker for you. He's lovely too."

Kasia tried to smile back, but her eyes were filled with tears.

"Thanks, Lydia," said Sally. Then she turned to the girls and put on a smile. "Right, everyone, end of drama. Let's get back on the yard, we're running late." And with that she walked out.

Dad gave Mum a quick kiss as she came back in with the ice pack, then he left too.

"Zoe and Amy, you stay behind for a moment, please," said Mum, as the others trooped out.

Seeing how worried they looked made me feel awful. Even worse, Mum told them off for covering for me. I tried to tell her they didn't want to and that it was all my fault, but she wouldn't listen.

When she left the kitchen, they were both upset and Zoe was close to tears.

"I'm so sorry," I told them. "I wish I hadn't done it, and I shouldn't have persuaded you to cover for me either."

They both said it was OK, but I could see that they were still shaken up about it all.

So that's what happened. I feel AWFUL about upsetting Kasia, and getting Zoe and Amy into trouble. And I can't stop worrying about Tally. The vet's coming later, and all these terrible thoughts keep whirling round in my head. Like, *What if it's not just a strain? What if he's really hurt his leg and has to have an operation? He'd be heartbroken if he could never canter again! What if he can't be ridden any more AT ALL?* I feel so sick thinking that and my heart won't stop hammering.

If my ankle's OK, Mum's putting me on yard duties all day tomorrow as punishment. "If any of the other girls did this they'd be on yard jobs too and you're no different, young lady," she snapped, as she pressed the ice pack to my ankle. "That's if they were lucky. That's if they weren't sent home."

I feel bad that Magic will be expecting me to come and tack up with the others after the lecture this afternoon. He'll be left all alone and not know why. I don't want him to think he's done anything wrong. Hopefully Lydia will turn him out, so he won't be stuck in the barn by himself. I wanted to limp down there and turn him out myself, but I know there wasn't even any point in asking, not with Mum so cross with me.

Oh, she's got jobs for me NOW, too. Shelling peas here at the table. Better get started.

Tuesday night, writing this in bed

Well, the vet's been, and Tally does only have a strain and some bruising, THANK GOODNESS, though I hate to think of him having any injury at all. He's had an ice pack on it, same as me, and bute powder in his food to bring down the inflammation. My own ankle's not too bad now – a bit sore, but I can get my boot on again.

Mum told me Kasia did well on Cracker, but that she was still obviously upset about Tally. Kasia seemed OK-ish towards me at teatime, and so did Elizabeth and Evie, but Irenka and her friends just acted like I wasn't there. I'm actually quite glad I'm not riding with them tomorrow.

Zoe and Amy were still a bit gloomy at tea, especially around Mum, but during pudding Amy was doing an impression of herself getting loads of stuff wrong in their quiz on points of the horse and Zoe was laughing. I started laughing too, and soon we were all chatting together normally, and I told them again how sorry I was. Then when everyone was playing volleyball after tea Mum picked them for her team, and that cheered them up even more.

After lights out, I couldn't get up to Amy's bunk to share her pick 'n' mix (we didn't even bother trying to wait till midnight again!), so she and Zoe both came and sat on my bed instead.

"What are you going to do about Tally now?" Zoe asked.

I sighed. I'd been thinking all afternoon (well, I had plenty of time by myself and a mountain of peas to shell). I'd worked some things out, but I still found it hard to say them aloud. I took a deep breath. "I think Mum's right, Tally is too small for me," I admitted. "And *of course* I don't expect him to never be ridden again, and *of course* I'd rather he stayed at Pony Camp than be sold on. But it's just so hard to let him go. He's my best friend. We're a team. I know I have to, though, somehow."

There, I'd said it. And then I got a surprise because I suddenly started crying (something I *never* normally do). Zoe put her arm round me and Amy gave me the last cola bottle in the bag.

"Oh, I've messed everything up, with everyone!" I wailed. "Tally's injured, Kasia's upset, the other girls are in a huge mood with me, and I don't think I've ever *seen* Mum so angry."

"It'll be OK," said Zoe.

"Thanks, but I can't see how," I sniffled. "I'll just have to try and put things right in the morning. As best I can, anyway."

Zoe and Amy stayed with me till I'd calmed down a bit, and then they each gave me a big hug and got back into their beds before Mum could come and tell us off. I snuggled down under my duvet, but I couldn't sleep and every time I moved my ankle started throbbing again. My mind wouldn't stop whirring, thinking about everything. I thought writing in this diary might help, and perhaps it has, because

Wednesday morning, first thing

My ankle still feels a bit sore, but I'm determined
not to show it. As soon as I've got dressed I'm
going to ask Sally if I can walk Tally up and
down the lane, before I have to start on my
yard duties. If I can get his strained muscle eased
off and loose enough, maybe Kasia will
be able to ride him later.

    I need to see Magic too, to tell him how
sorry I am about everything. I realized last night
that he's probably missing his old rider as much
as I'm missing Tally, so I should have been giving
him lots of extra cuddles, not
ignoring him, poor thing. I've
been so wrapped up in my
own problems I didn't even

poor
MAGIC!

think about that before. Oh, I just
can't believe how uncaring I've been!
I really hope he'll give me another chance.

4.05p.m. — on the bench outside the yard office, waiting for Mum to come and check my jobs

Irenka and Kasia saw me walking Tally up and down this morning, and Irenka got the wrong idea and thought I was taking over again. She gave me an even chillier look than yesterday and stalked off. Kasia followed, but I called out, "Kasia, wait, please!"

I didn't think she would, but she stopped and turned to face me. "I really am so sorry for what I did yesterday," I gabbled. "I feel awful that you had to miss out on riding Tally because of me. That's why I'm trying to get him loosened up now — I'm hoping you might be able to ride him today."

Kasia gave me a long stare. Then she said, "Can I help?"

I grinned with relief. "Yeah, course."

So we walked Tally up
and down together
(I gave her the lead
rope to hold, of
course). She asked
me loads of questions
about him and it's
obvious she really cares.

Tally's leg seemed fine to me, a bit stiff at first
maybe. But of course it was down to Mum to
decide whether Kasia could ride him today.

I had all my fingers crossed when she came
to have a look at him. And luckily she said he's
fine to be ridden. Hooray!

I was hoping Mum would let *me* ride instead
of doing chores, so I could spend more time
with Magic. But when I asked she just said,
"Dream on, Millie. Get yourself a spade."

I pulled a face, but then I went and got
started — no point being miserable about it!

Here's my jobs list:

1. Muck out (not just skip out) FOUR stables, on my OWN.

2. Poo-pick the lower field (yes, all of it!).

3. Put a big pile of sweaty numnahs on to wash (yurgh!).

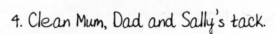

4. Clean Mum, Dad and Sally's tack.

5. Sweep the yard.

Well, I did everything! It took all day, just about, and when I'd finished, the stables and field and tack were spotless. I even hung the numnahs out on the line and by the time I'd finished with the broom, there wasn't a single bit of straw on the yard.

I only stopped once – to give Magic a big hug and tell him how sorry I am and how I hope we'll be a team from now on. He nuzzled into me so I think I'm forgiven, thank goodness!

Oh, here's Mum. But instead of inspecting my work, she wants me to come into the kitchen with her. I wonder what's going on…

Ten mins later, in the kitchen by myself – IN SHOCK!

When I walked in, Dad was here. There were two half-drunk mugs of tea on the table, so I knew they'd been chatting about something. They seemed really serious and my heart started thumping. "What's going on?" I asked, collapsing into a chair.

"We've been giving it a lot of thought, and based on the week so far your dad and I don't think Magic's the right pony for you," Mum replied. "We hoped you'd make a good team, but you're obviously not keen on the idea."

I tried to protest, but Dad cut me off. "From what Sally says, you have no rapport with him and you don't seem to have any feel for what he needs. And in the bit of the lesson that I saw, well, you could have helped him over those jumps, but you didn't even try."

"That's because I was riding badly *on purpose!*" I cried. "It was part of my plan to keep Tally. But I understand now that I can't."

Mum rolled her eyes at Dad. They obviously didn't believe me. And now I was going to lose Magic.

That's when I realized how fond I'd got of him. Yes, after only two days. Just like Kasia with Tally and all the other Pony Camp girls with their ponies. "Please, Mum," I begged. "I really, *really* want Magic."

"Millie, it's OK, you don't have to say that,"
Mum said, more gently. "I know we've been
angry about how you've behaved, but
pretending you want Magic won't help things.
We think it's best if you don't have a pony for a
while. You can ride the ones here and get over
Tally in your own time. I'll take Magic back and
explain that it hasn't worked out. Magic's such a
great pony he'll easily find another home."

I gasped. My mouth went dry and I felt sick.
This couldn't be happening. I'd been so stupid!
I'd messed everything up and now it was too
late to put it right. "But I promise you, I *do* want
Magic!" I cried. "You were right all along. We'd
be a great team. I'll prove it. Please, let me
prove it!"

Mum and Dad glanced at each other. They
didn't look convinced.

Dad gave me a long hard look. I stared back
at him, willing him to give me and Magic

another go. "OK, win the Chase Me Charlie
in Friday's gymkhana with him and he's yours,"
he said.

"WHAT?!" I shrieked. "But the others are
really good riders, ask Sally! And Zuzanna's got
Charm, the best jumper here!"

"You asked for a chance and I'm giving you
one," said Dad.

"But it's impossible!" I protested. "Jumping is
Magic's weak point. There's no way we'll win.
Anything else, Dad, and I'll do it. I'll do yard jobs
for a month! I'll wash up every day for the rest
of the summer! Anything! Please!"

Even Mum said, "Johnny, are you sure about
this?"

But Dad wouldn't change his mind. "I'm not
impressed with the way you've been acting this
week, Millie," he said sternly. "To be given a
pony, something I could only dream of at your
age, and to behave the way you have – it's

ungrateful and spoilt. Do you have any idea how hard we've worked to save up for Magic? I'm really not sure you deserve him now, or any pony, come to that! Magic's great, and he should have a rider who'll really care about him."

"But I *do* care about him!" I wailed. I almost started crying, but I swallowed back the tears. "Fine," I said, "we'll take the challenge!"

We'll take the challenge!

"Good," said Dad, then he stood up, squeezed Mum's shoulders and walked out. After that, Mum had to make a couple of phone calls, so I've been writing this.

Oh, she's just come back in and said she's ready to check my chores.

Wednesday evening,
hanging out in my room.
Me, Amy and Zoe are all lying
on our beds, writing in our diaries

Well, the girls' lesson had finished so the yard
was all messed up again by the time Mum
looked at it. While she inspected the tack room
and stables (and took a call in the office), I
swept it again, to make it as spotless as before.
She came out smiling, saying how impressed she
was with everything I'd done – phew!

"Good. I wanted you to be," I said. "I can't
believe how spoilt I've been! I really *am* sorry."

Mum gave me a half smile. "I know," she said.
"And I've been thinking, you must have been
desperate to keep Tally to try something so
crazy. Why didn't you tell me how you felt?"

I sighed. "I did try, four times yesterday, and
loads before Magic came! But you wouldn't

67

listen, you were always too busy."

Mum looked startled at first, then she said, "I'm sorry, love, things get so hectic with the girls here, but still, I should have taken the time to listen to you. Not that it's any excuse for what you did!"

"I know it's not," I said quickly. "I just got so angry and upset. I wasn't thinking straight. I'll never put a pony or myself in danger like that again. I can't bear to think what might have happened to Tally, it could have been far more serious than it was."

Mum squeezed my shoulders. "Let's put it behind us, shall we?"

I hugged her waist. "Thanks."

After a moment, she said, "Right then, next…"

I cut in. "Let me guess. More shelling peas? Extra poo-picking?"

Mum laughed. "Actually, the tea's all prepared, so I thought we could go out on the cross-country course. You ought to get back in the saddle as soon as possible after a fall."

Wow! "Really? Thanks, Mum!" I cried. "Me and Magic need to get lots of jumping practice in before the Chase Me Charlie on Friday. *And* hope that luck's on our side. *Lots* of it. No chance Dad will change his mind about me having to win, I suppose?"

Mum just raised an eyebrow at me. We both knew the answer to that. "Better get cracking then," I said.

So that's what we did. Mum tacked up her horse, Bonny, and I got Magic ready. As I buckled up his girth, I told him about Dad's challenge, then added, "I know it seems impossible, but we've got to try." He snorted and turned his head to nudge me, so I think he wants us to stay together too.

We trotted up the lane, and warmed up
with some walk, trot and canter round the field.
Mum suggested that I start by working Magic
over a single jump (the log pile), because it's
fairly low, then circling round between the
double log jumps and the hedge. He did refuse
twice, but I just carried on, and gave him lots of
encouragement and an extra squeeze before he
took off. I also did as Mum
said and focused
forward past the
jump, as if it wasn't
even there.

Go Magic!

And guess what?

He went over!

And again, and a third time!

When we stopped for a rest, I leaned
forward on to his neck and gave him loads of
praise. The cross-country jumps are far more
solid than the poles we use in the manège, so

Magic needed even MORE bravery to tackle that log pile. Maybe a bit of my confidence rubbed off on him too, because then when we tried the hedge, tyres and ditch as a mini-course, we cleared them. (OK, not perfectly, but never mind!)

I started to think that with lots of practice we might stand some chance in the Chase Me Charlie on Friday, but we're a long way off yet! If the hedge had been a pole we'd have had it down both times, and one of Magic's hind hooves hit the tyres once too, so we'd have knocked a pole off then as well. And as for the ditch, Magic jumped it beautifully but, being a hole in the ground filled with water, it hardly counts as a *height*!

I didn't even *attempt* the gate at first, just went round beside it instead, because it's pretty high and I thought Magic might refuse it. But then Mum offered to give me a lead, so we had a go, and yes, we got over, *just*! I stopped there, as I wanted to end on a positive note. The Chase Me Charlie might go up even *higher* than the gate, though, especially with Charm in the running, and Irenka riding Flame so well.

On the way back, I started chatting to Mum about how, *if* by some miracle we win the comp on Friday and I get to keep Magic, we could go in for the cross-country at the Crewkerne Show this year. Then I suddenly stopped, feeling bad because I always do that show with Tally.

Mum must have known what I was thinking because she said, "You know, it's OK to be excited about Magic. I gave Tally to someone else this week for a reason. I hoped you'd feel that, as he wasn't being left out, you could get on and enjoy yourself too."

I was startled. "Oh! So you were actually trying to *help* by giving him to Kasia?"

Mum gave me a shocked look. "Believe it or not, Millie, yes!" she cried. "I don't set out to make you unhappy, you know!"

I grinned. "I *suppose* not!"

Mum laughed. "Watch it, cheeky madam!"

When I was untacking and brushing Magic down in the yard I gave him a great big hug and told him how well he'd done. He seemed really proud of himself as he nuzzled into my chest. We've got to stay together, we've just *got* to. But I still don't know how on earth we're going to win the Chase Me Charlie.

MAGIC

And there's something else I need to do. After yesterday I wouldn't dare go behind Mum's back so I'll have to ask her straight out. Here goes…

Wednesday night, in bed after lights out

Well, I asked Mum if I could go and spend some time with Tally and she said yes. She made me a flask of hot chocolate, and I took an apple and carrot for him. He's stabled again tonight, just to be extra-careful of his leg. It was great to be with him. I gave him loads of hugs and pats, and he nuzzled me back.

Then I started chatting to him about all the fun times we've had together. When I said, "Remember that time you dragged me straight through a hedge on that hack?" he gave me a look as if to say, "Which one?" And it's true, there have been loads! Me and Tally might not have had much style, or patience (or BRAKES!), but we've had the most BRILLIANT time together.

As I ruffled his mane, I tried to explain about getting too big for him and how I'd love to ride him for ever but I just can't. "I bet you'll have a great time as a Pony Camp pony," I told him. "It means we can still hang out together, and I know now that the Pony Camp girls really will care about you, like Kasia does. You'll make lots of new friends…" I had to stop for a second to wipe my nose on my sleeve – OK, so I was crying a tiny bit by then. "And none of your new riders will know you're going to cart them through the bushes. Think how much fun that will be!" I giggled and Tally snorted and leaned into me. "And if any Pony Camp girl *is* mean to you, she'll be getting a dose of slugs in the bed!" I promised him.

Amy and Zoe appeared then, with their pyjamas tucked into their riding boots. "Your mum sent us to get you," said Amy. "Do you like our new fashion?" They both started doing model-ish poses and giggling. But then, "Oh," said Zoe, peering at me, "You've been crying."

"A bit," I admitted. "I've just been telling Tally how much fun he's going to have as a Pony Camper. I think he's OK about it now."

Zoe put her arm round me. "Are you?" she asked, as Amy gave Tally a pat.

"Yes, I really think I am now," I told them. "I mean, it'll take time to get used to, but I know it's for the best. Thanks for being such good friends and helping me to see that."

"No worries," said Amy. They both suddenly hugged me at once, and I hugged them back. Then I gave Tally an extra big hug.

As we wandered back to the house, linking arms, I said, "Now I've got to somehow pull off a miracle and win the Chase Me Charlie on Friday or it's bye-bye Magic, too."

They just looked awkward and didn't say, "You'll be fine," or anything. They know as well as I do that it's a near-impossible challenge.

We came back inside just as Mum was making hot chocolate for everyone. As we all sat round the table I tried to join in with the laughing and chatting, but I couldn't stop thinking about the challenge ahead.

No time to think about that now, though. I can hear Mum on the stairs. Night, night!

77

Thursday lunchtime

I just realized I didn't even *notice* my ankle when I got up this morning, so it must be better.

Irenka and her friends are still being a bit off with me on the yard, but I've got something far more important to worry about – keeping Magic!

Luckily, we did jumping in our lesson – some fairly high uprights and a couple of spreads, so me and Magic got another chance to try and improve before the Chase Me Charlie. Although he refused the first couple of times, I kept encouraging him and got my leg on strongly to urge him forward. That gave him the confidence to be a bit braver and we got going after that.

But we won't have time to do that tomorrow – two refusals and we're out of the competition, and I lose Magic. Still, we're doing OK, and Zoe and Amy have been trying to help me think positive. They really are fab mates!

After tea

This afternoon we had a talk on road safety
and first aid, and then we went out for a hack.
Zoe and Amy were so excited, it made me
excited too. But then when we were all walking
up the lane, I found myself next to Irenka. It
was a bit awkward at first, with everyone
chatting and us two just going along in silence.
Finally I got up the courage to say, "I really am
sorry about taking Tally out. And I never meant
to upset Kasia."

Irenka didn't reply and I thought she was still
ignoring me, but finally she said, "OK, let's forget
about it."

Well, phew! What a relief!

We turned on to a track and Sally started
her talk about having a gentle canter up the hill
if we wanted to. Irenka grinned at me. "Come
on, race you!" she whispered. She kicked Flame

79

on and, of course, one tiny touch is all it takes to get *her* going, so they absolutely bolted off.

Usually I would have taken off too, but with all the trouble I've been in, I decided I'd better not. But then *Magic* went galloping after them! And well, once we'd started there was no point pulling him up, so I leaned forward and really encouraged him to go for it. In seconds we were neck and neck with Flame. "Yee-ha!" Irenka shouted, making us both laugh.

Then, eeeeekkk! We really had to put the brakes on hard at the top of the hill or the ponies would have been over the hedge and trampling the uncut barley in the next field ... and I would have been on poo-picking punishment for the rest of the summer!

When the others caught us up, we were both gasping and giggling. There was no point in Irenka even trying to pretend she'd gone off accidentally. But luckily Sally didn't give us too much of a telling-off!

So maybe Magic does have a bit of ρΙℤℤΑℤℤ! after all. Perhaps we suit each other even better than I thought! And speaking of ρΙℤℤΑℤℤ!, Kasia did the canter too, and she and Tally were one of the first pairs to catch us up! And she managed to stop him pretty well – as well as *anyone* can, that is!

On the way back we had a couple of goes at jumping this log in a field. That started a friendly row between Irenka, Zuzanna and Angelika about which of them was going to win the Chase Me Charlie tomorrow. None of them even *considered* that Amy or I or one of the Group A girls could win. And to be honest, they're probably right. What am I going to do?! I can't lose Magic now. **ARGH!**

Gotta go, Evie and Elizabeth have finished their clearing-up duty, and they want me to set up the karaoke machine. I can't believe it's the girls' last night already!

Friday — quickly writing this during our morning break

It was so much fun after tea, because we ended up having a big karaoke disco party in the games room. Me, Zoe and Amy sang together really loudly and got everyone dancing.

Then after lights out, us three were whispering and messing around so much that I managed to forget about Dad's challenge for a while. I remembered the second I woke up this morning, though, and thinking about it made me feel really sick. On the yard I made loads of fuss of Magic (after all, it's probably our last day together). In the end, Lydia said, "Millie, could you please stop *hugging* that pony and get him tacked up!"

In our lesson this morning I was hoping for more jumping practice, but instead we went over the lateral work we'd done on Tuesday. Everyone had really got the hang of it this time (even naughty Mischief, with Amy to guide him). Sally said how well we'd done this week, and we all gave her a clap for being such a fab instructor. Luckily, she noticed my pleading looks and she set up a jump to finish off with. Me and Magic are jumping as well as Amy and Angelika, but Zuzanna and Irenka are still better than us. We'll really need a lot of luck to win this afternoon. But we *have* to, somehow. I can't even bear to *think* about losing Magic now.

Friday evening, and everyone's gone home

It's always kind of nice to have my room back to myself, but it feels lonely as well, too big and empty. I just want to finish off my diary before bed – I'd never have guessed this week would be so amazing, exciting and scary!

Did I get to keep Magic? Well… Here's the whole story…

I was getting more and more nervous as we got the ponies ready for the gymkhana. Zoe was plaiting ribbons into Fisher's lovely long mane, and Amy was busy with the glitter hoof gel on Mischief, but my fingers were trembling so much I could barely brush Magic down.

As the parents began to arrive, there was lots of excitement and chatter. We played some other gymkhana games before the Chase Me Charlie, and everyone gathered by the fence to cheer us on. When Zoe won the ball and bucket race, and Amy came first in the stepping stones, I gave them both an extra-big cheer. Magic and I didn't win anything, though — I couldn't really concentrate properly and I don't think he could either. After what felt like for ever it was time for the Chase Me Charlie. Our future was about to be decided.

As Sally was setting up the jump, my mates rode up beside me. "Good luck, Mil," said Zoe.

"Yeah, go for it," Amy added. "You *can* win this."

"Thanks," I said, trying to think positive too.

The first pole was barely off the ground and we all jumped it, no problem. The next couple of rounds were fine too. Then Evie and Elizabeth bowed out, seeing as they only started jumping this week. We all gave them a big clap

and cheer for having a go, and they looked
really pleased with themselves.

After two more rounds, Zoe had the pole
down. Everyone went,
"Oooh!" and "Never
mind," but she was
just grinning at me!

Then, well, I don't
know what happened, but seconds after Amy
set off, there was a big crash and the pole and
one of the jump stands were on the floor. Amy
insisted later that cheeky Mischief had ploughed
straight through the jump and got them
knocked out – but I'm not so sure. I reckon she
did it on purpose to give me more chance of
winning. She swears she didn't, but... Well, I
guess I'll never find out!

I had a lucky break in the next round when
Jewel rushed at the jump and had the pole
down. Everyone gasped – they couldn't believe

Angelika was out so early in the competition.
And then Tally typically (and helpfully!) did a
huge leap over, knocked the pole off, and nearly
sent Kasia flying. Luckily, she managed to grab
his mane and hang on, but what a little monkey!

So there we were – me, Irenka and Zuzanna
– and I felt like bowing out, running up here to
my room, sticking my head under the covers
and having a big cry about losing Magic. But I
didn't, of course. Helping him to be brave has
made me remember how brave *I* am too, and
I knew we had to keep going. I took a deep
breath and made myself think extra positive as
Sally put the top pole up another notch.

Zuzanna and Charm sailed over. It was like
they weren't even trying. Then it was our turn.
I gave Magic a pat. "Come on, boy, I know we
can do this," I told him. We trotted a circle,
went into canter on the straight and…

We were over!

"Whoopee!" I cried, then leaned forward to give Magic a big hug.

When Irenka and Flame went over I held my breath, willing them to knock the pole off, but they cleared it.

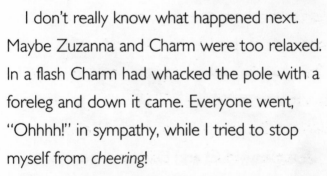

And up it went.

I don't really know what happened next. Maybe Zuzanna and Charm were too relaxed. In a flash Charm had whacked the pole with a foreleg and down it came. Everyone went, "Ohhhh!" in sympathy, while I tried to stop myself from *cheering*!

So in the end it was between me and Irenka. She grinned at me, and I forced myself to smile back. Her friends and family all started cheering her on, and Mum, Dad, Zoe and Amy began chanting for me.

My heart pounding, I nudged Magic into trot then canter, focused past the jump and over we went … with a CLUNK.

My heart sank – Magic had nudged the pole with a hind leg. I glanced behind us, expecting to see it on the ground, but no – it was still up! Wobbling, but still up! I stared hard at it, willing it to stay put. After what felt like for ever it came to a stop!

still UP!

Zoe, Amy, Mum and Dad were going wild, cheering for us. Then Irenka's family started chanting her name as she set off and picked up trot, then canter. Flame seemed to speed up very suddenly, then they were up, and CLUNK, one of her hind hooves hit the pole too, exactly

as Magic's had. Irenka looked back anxiously and
I stared hard at the pole. Wobble. Still up.
Wobble. Still up. It felt like for ever. Then …
THUD.

The pole was down.

I could hardly take it in, but … we'd won!

All I could do was hug Magic's neck, as tears
of relief ran down my cheeks. "I'm so proud of
you!" I cried. Magic, MY pony Magic, snorted
and shook his head, and I knew he
was proud of himself, too.
Yes, we'd shown a lot of
determination and tried hard.
But in the end it was that little
bit of luck that clinched it for us.

We all stood in a line with our ponies, and
Sally handed out the rosettes as everyone
clapped and cheered. Zoe and Amy tied theirs
to Fisher and Mischief's bridles, and their
parents took about a million photos.

"And for the Chase Me Charlie, Millie and Magic!" Sally announced. I was beaming as I shook her hand and accepted our red rosette.

Winning something in the end of week gymkhana isn't exactly a big deal for me usually, but this time I was just as excited as the other girls. I tied the rosette to Magic's bridle with pride and gave him a big pat. And suddenly Dad was there, clicking away, taking pictures of *us*!

Everyone gave us a big clap, and Mum came over and wrapped me up in a huge hug. Then she announced that there was tea and juice on offer in the kitchen. The grown-ups began to head over to the house, and Lydia led us girls and ponies off to the barn.

As I came back out, Dad strode up to me. "Well done, sweetheart," he said, "I'm so proud

of you, of both of you! When I saw how stiff
the competition was out there I did get a bit
worried, I have to admit. But I always believed
you could win if you really set your mind to it."

"Thanks," I said, then I added, "I can't believe
you were going to take Magic away from me if
I hadn't won!"

He looked thoughtful. "Hmm, well, I'm not
sure I would have done, in the end."

"What?!" I shrieked. "So I went through all
that for nothing?!" I nudged him hard with my
elbow. "Well, thanks very much!"

"It wasn't for nothing," he said firmly.
"I wanted to make sure you were serious about
Magic, and the competition
gave you the chance to
prove you were.
You've earned him
now, and I know you
really want him."

"Oh, well, thanks for believing me, at last!"
I grumbled. But I couldn't help smiling. Dad
doesn't give out compliments very often. What
he'd said meant a lot to me.

"Now Magic's starting to jump good heights,
you could do some showjumping," he said then.

"*Me?*" I gasped. "Not likely! I've got about
as much style and precision on horseback as,
well, YOU!"

He laughed at that. "Well, maybe Magic
could teach you a thing or two in that
department, and you can keep on helping him
to be brave and bold!"

That gave me an idea. "Hey, maybe we could
go in for a one-day event! We both have our
weak spots, but together we're a great team!"

"Now, that's a good idea, Millie," Dad said,
with a grin. "Me and your mum *obviously* didn't
think of that when we suggested giving Magic
a go."

"Oh, you think you're so smart!" I teased. "And how annoying that you were right!"

Just before home-time, I went up to the field with the other girls to turn out the ponies. We all gave our ponies big hugs, then me and Amy had to give Zoe a big hug because she was really upset about leaving Fisher, and I had to promise to e-mail her new pics of him every week. I feel SO lucky that I live here. I couldn't bear to leave Magic. Not now that we're a team. Hmm, team Millie and Magic, it's got a nice ring to it. And I just know we're going to have loads of adventures together!

To Sarah, a fab vet and a super sister-in-law
— with love xx

With special thanks to our cover stars,
Jess and Connor, pony guru Janet Rising
and our brill photographer, Zoe Cannon.

www.kellymckain.co.uk

STRIPES PUBLISHING
An imprint of Magi Publications
1 The Coda Centre, 189 Munster Road, London SW6 6AW

A paperback original
First published in Great Britain in 2010

Text copyright © Kelly McKain, 2010
Illustrations copyright © Mandy Stanley, 2010
Cover photograph copyright © Zoe Cannon, 2010

ISBN: 978-1-84715-135-3

The right of Kelly McKain and Mandy Stanley to be identified as the author
and illustrator of this work respectively has been asserted by them in
accordance with the Copyright, Designs and Patents Act, 1988.

All rights reserved.

This book is sold subject to the condition that it shall not, by way of trade or otherwise, be
lent, resold, hired out, or otherwise circulated without the publisher's prior consent in any
form of binding or cover other than that in which it is published and without a similar
condition, including this condition, being imposed upon the subsequent purchaser.

A CIP catalogue record for this book is available from the British Library.

Printed in the UK

2 4 6 8 10 9 7 5 3 1